Douk-Douk Island
Philip's Hole
Field of Chasms
Kite's Circus
Fork Village
MAIN ROAD: CHICHINIA ROAD
Border
wbottom
illage
Damien's House
Forest

Anne Simon

THE EMPRESS CIXTISIS

Fantagraphics Books

Posters were put up across Barbarann: Get rich in Chichinia! So the men set off to make their fortune, but most of them never returned...

Some say that Cixtisis, the Great Empress, is not unrelated with their disappearance.

Suffragette City, Capital of Barbarann
The mail carrier does her daily morning route and stops at Queen Aglaia's palace.
CLING
CLING
HELLO! A PACKAGE FOR HER MAJESTY.
YES?
HER MAJESTY IS IN THE SHOWER. I'M HER SECRETARY. I TAKE HER MAIL.
SIGN HERE, PLEASE.
WELL... THANKS.
I WAS WONDERING... ABOUT MY HUSBAND... IF YOU HAD ANY NEWS...
AGLAIA IS TAKING CARE OF THE MATTER.
GOODBYE.

AGLAIA! THEY JUST DELIV-ERED A PACKAGE FOR YOU.
NOK NOK
YOU CAN COME IN, SIMONE!
THERE'S NO SENDER.
OPEN IT!
IT'S MOST LIKELY FROM A FAN.
...
WELL I NEVER! A LETTER FROM DAMIEN...
WE HAVEN'T HEARD FROM HIM SINCE HE LOST YOUR CROWN.
HE DIDN'T LOSE IT— HE STOLE IT! TO SELL, NO DOUBT.
NO... LOOK.
HERE IT IS!
OH!
LET ME SEE!
IT REALLY IS MY CROWN. MY DARLING CROWN!
WHAT COULD HAVE HAPPENED?

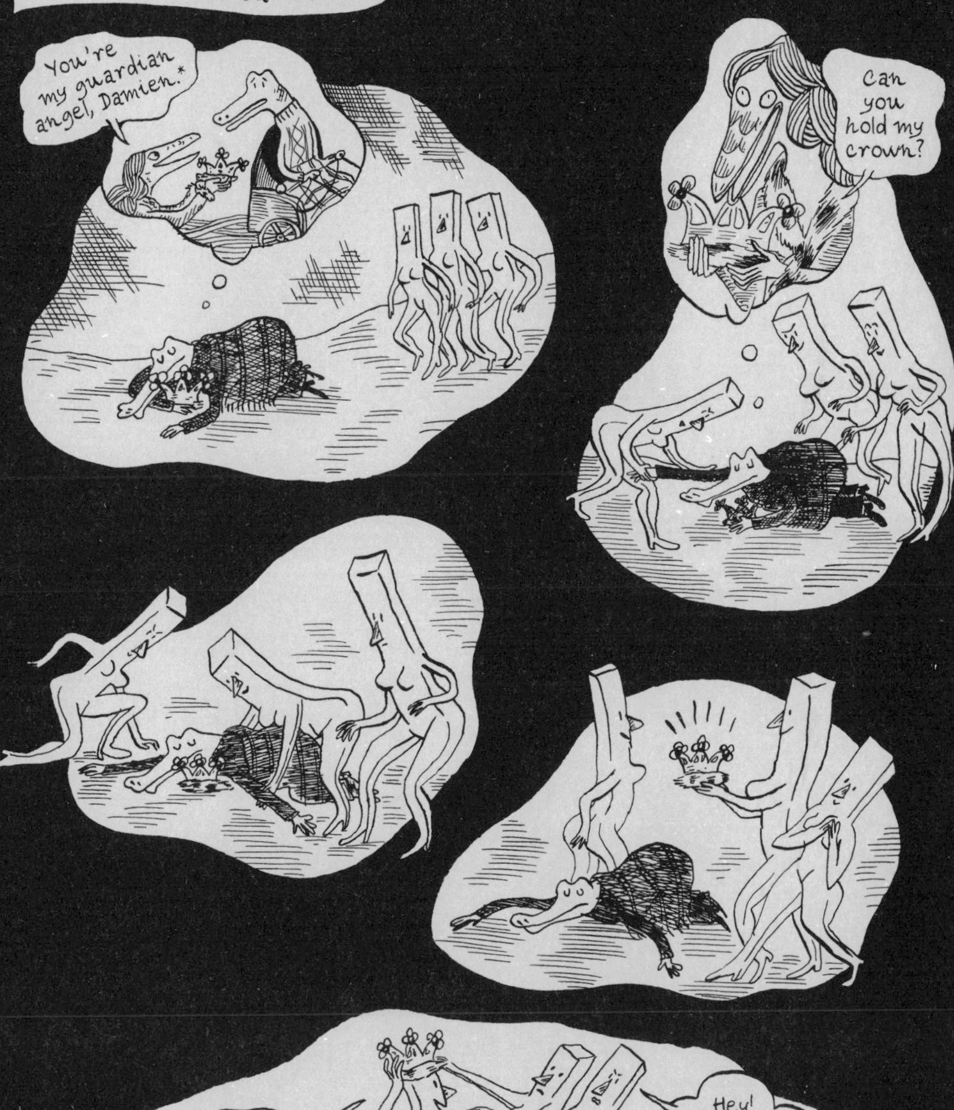

* See "THE SONG OF AGLAIA"

Someone stole Queen Aglaia's crown!

Damien the cook was supposed to be watching it, but he lost it!

Someone stole Queen Aglaia's crown!

Crocodile Blues

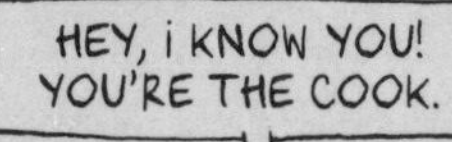
HEY, i KNOW YOU! YOU'RE THE COOK.

i'M NOT THE COOK.
i'M NOTHING NOW.

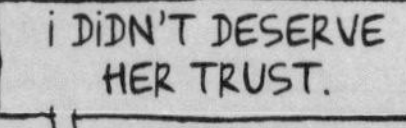
i DiDN'T DESERVE HER TRUST.

i SEE YOU A LOT AROUND HERE.

i KNOW YOU'RE DOiNG ALL YOU CAN TO FiX YOUR MiSTAKE AND FiND THE CROWN.

i CAN HELP YOU iF YOU WANT.

MY NAME IS PERSEPHONE.
I'M DAMIEN.
DAMIEN THE GOOD-FOR-NOTHING...
OH! DON'T SAY THAT!
COME ON.
I HAVE MY OWN WORRIES TOO, RIGHT NOW, SO YOU KNOW.
BUT DO I LOOK LIKE I'M AT A FUNERAL?
NO!
SO WE'LL GET OFF OUR BUTTS AND LOOK FOR THE CROWN, BUT STRATEGICALLY!
WHAT'S YOUR STRATEGY?
WE SIT.
AND WE THINK.

LET'S SAY EVERYTHING THAT COMES TO MIND AND THEN WE'LL REVIEW.
I WANT FRIES.
INTERESTING.
WHEN AGLAIA ENTRUSTED HER CROWN TO ME, I HAD JUST MADE HER FRIES.
SINCE THEN, I HAVEN'T STOPPED THINKING ABOUT THAT.
THE SMELL OF FRIED FOOD IS CLINGING TO MY NOSTRILS.
THE NIGHT THE CROWN WAS STOLEN FROM ME, I HAD A FUNNY DREAM.
I FELT LIKE I WAS SURROUNDED BY GIANT FRIES. IT REEKED OF FRY OIL.
MAYBE IT WASN'T A DREAM, DAMIEN.

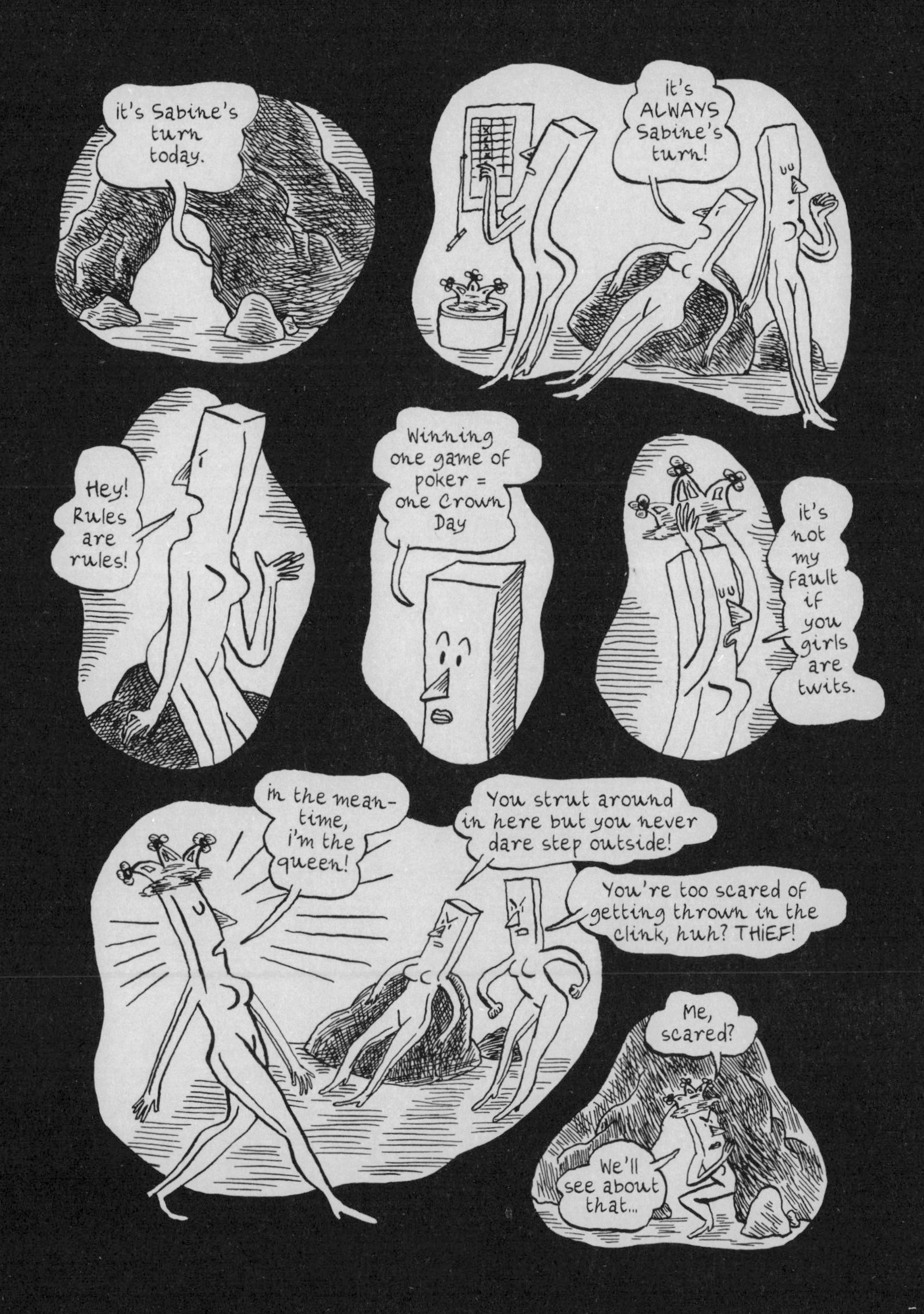
it's Sabine's turn today.
it's ALWAYS Sabine's turn!
Hey! Rules are rules!
Winning one game of poker = one Crown Day
it's not my fault if you girls are twits.
in the mean-time, i'm the queen!
You strut around in here but you never dare step outside!
You're too scared of getting thrown in the clink, huh? THIEF!
Me, scared?
We'll see about that...

YOU'RE TAKING ME FOR A RIDE.
I'M NOT!
A GANG OF KLEPTO FRIES? NO WAY!
I SAW THEM THE OTHER DAY.
THEY WERE STEALING A JAR OF MAYO FROM THE LOCAL GROCERY STORE.
I DIDN'T REPORT THEM. THAT'S NOT MY STYLE.
BUT THIS IS ABOUT THE QUEEN'S CROWN AND IT'S VERY SERIOUS!
APPARENTLY THEY WERE OFTEN SEEN DURING VON KRANTZ'S RULE.
HE MADE THEM INTO A FORMIDABLE ARMY.
WE CAN FIND MORE INFO WITH THIS.
THEY ALMOST ALL DISAPPEARED SINCE THEIR MASTER'S DEATH AND AGLAIA'S RISE TO POWER.
SEE, THAT'S WHAT THEY LOOK LIKE.

I'M SURPRISED YOU'VE NEVER HEARD OF THEM.
UM... UH... NO... I SWEAR.
LIAR.
SABINE?
SABINE!

GEEZ... SABINE.
YOU'RE IN LOVE WITH HER. YOU KNEW THAT SHE HAD STOLEN THE CROWN AND YOU DIDN'T WANT TO TURN HER IN, IS THAT IT?
NOT AT ALL!
YOU'RE A TERRIBLE LIAR.
DO YOU WANT TO TALK ABOUT IT, DAMIEN?
THERE'S NOTHING TO TELL.
BUT IT'S NICE OF YOU TO HELP ME, PERSEPHONE.
LET'S GO BACK. I'M HUNGRY.
I HAVE SOME ZUCCHINI AND EGGPLANT.
SOME ONIONS, TOO.
IF YOU WANT, I'LL TEACH YOU TO MAKE RATATOUILLE.
AND HEY, PUT DOWN THAT CROWN. I FEEL LIKE IT'S JINXED.

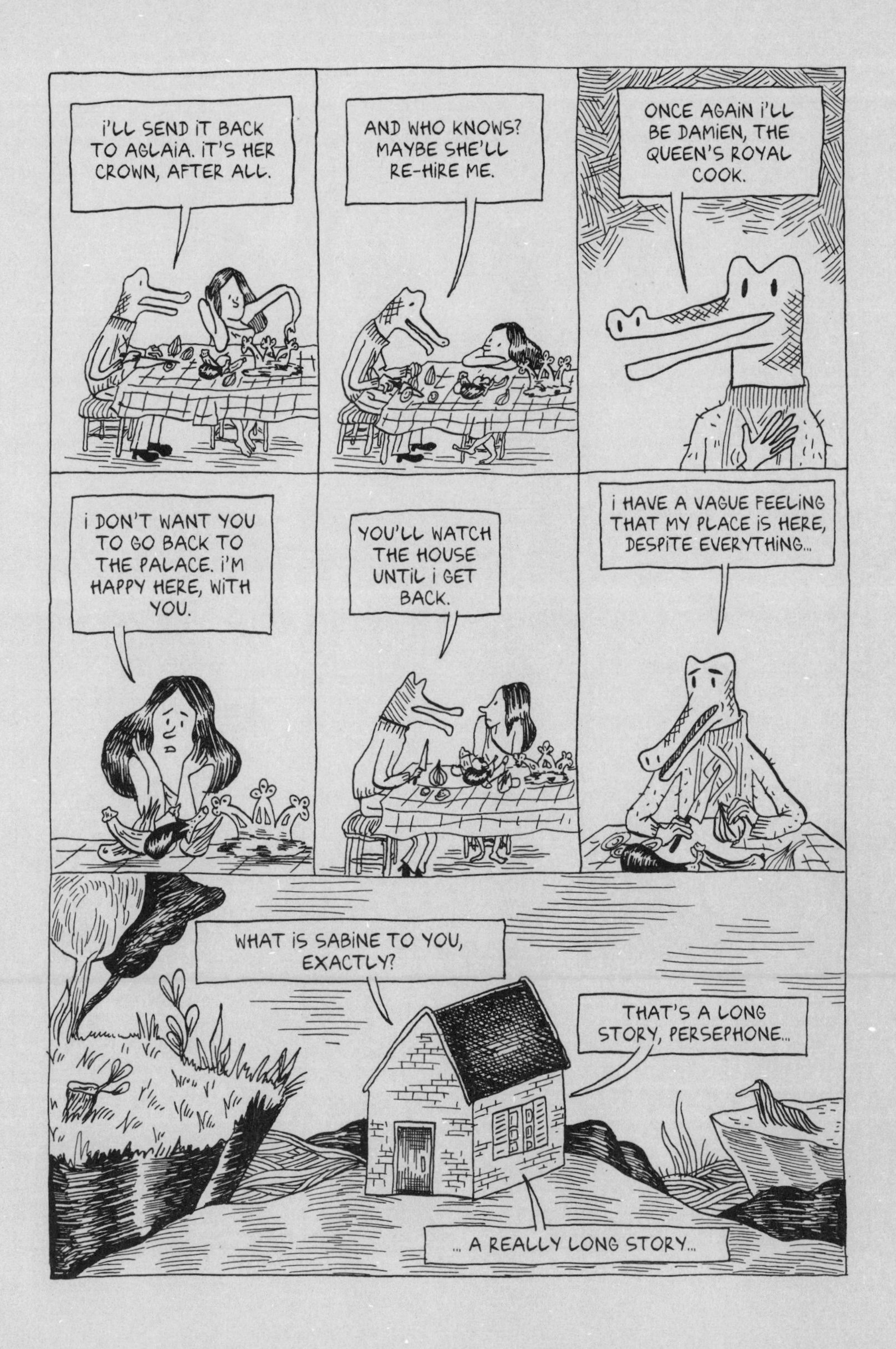
I'LL SEND IT BACK TO AGLAIA. IT'S HER CROWN, AFTER ALL.
AND WHO KNOWS? MAYBE SHE'LL RE-HIRE ME.
ONCE AGAIN I'LL BE DAMIEN, THE QUEEN'S ROYAL COOK.
I DON'T WANT YOU TO GO BACK TO THE PALACE. I'M HAPPY HERE, WITH YOU.
YOU'LL WATCH THE HOUSE UNTIL I GET BACK.
I HAVE A VAGUE FEELING THAT MY PLACE IS HERE, DESPITE EVERYTHING...
WHAT IS SABINE TO YOU, EXACTLY?
THAT'S A LONG STORY, PERSEPHONE...
... A REALLY LONG STORY...

HE LEFT A PHONE NUMBER.
IT WOULD BE NICE TO HAVE A MAN IN THE PALACE.
BUT CIXTISIS IS COMING. SHE'S GOING TO DEMAND...
EXACTLY! IT'LL SHUT HER TRAP.
DAMIEN IS A ROCK-SOLID ALIBI. AND HE'S HELPFUL. HE COOKS.
I'M GOING TO CALL HIM...
555...
NOT SO FAST!
05... 21...
RING-A-LING...
IT'S RINGING.
HELLO... DAMIEN? WHERE HAVE YOU BEEN HIDING? RETURN IMMEDIATELY... YES. I MISS YOUR FRIES.
AND HAVING A MAN AROUND HERE WOULDN'T HURT.
GREAT... THAT'S PERFECT, DAMIEN. SEE YOU SOON... YES, DAMIEN... OK... I'M HANGING UP, DAMIEN...
HE AGREED. HE'LL BE HERE TOMORROW.
GOOD OL' DAMIEN!
OOH! MY CROWN... THIS WILL GIVE ME THE HEART FOR THE WORK IN THE DAYS TO COME!

GOODBYE, PERSEPHONE.
COME BACK SOON.

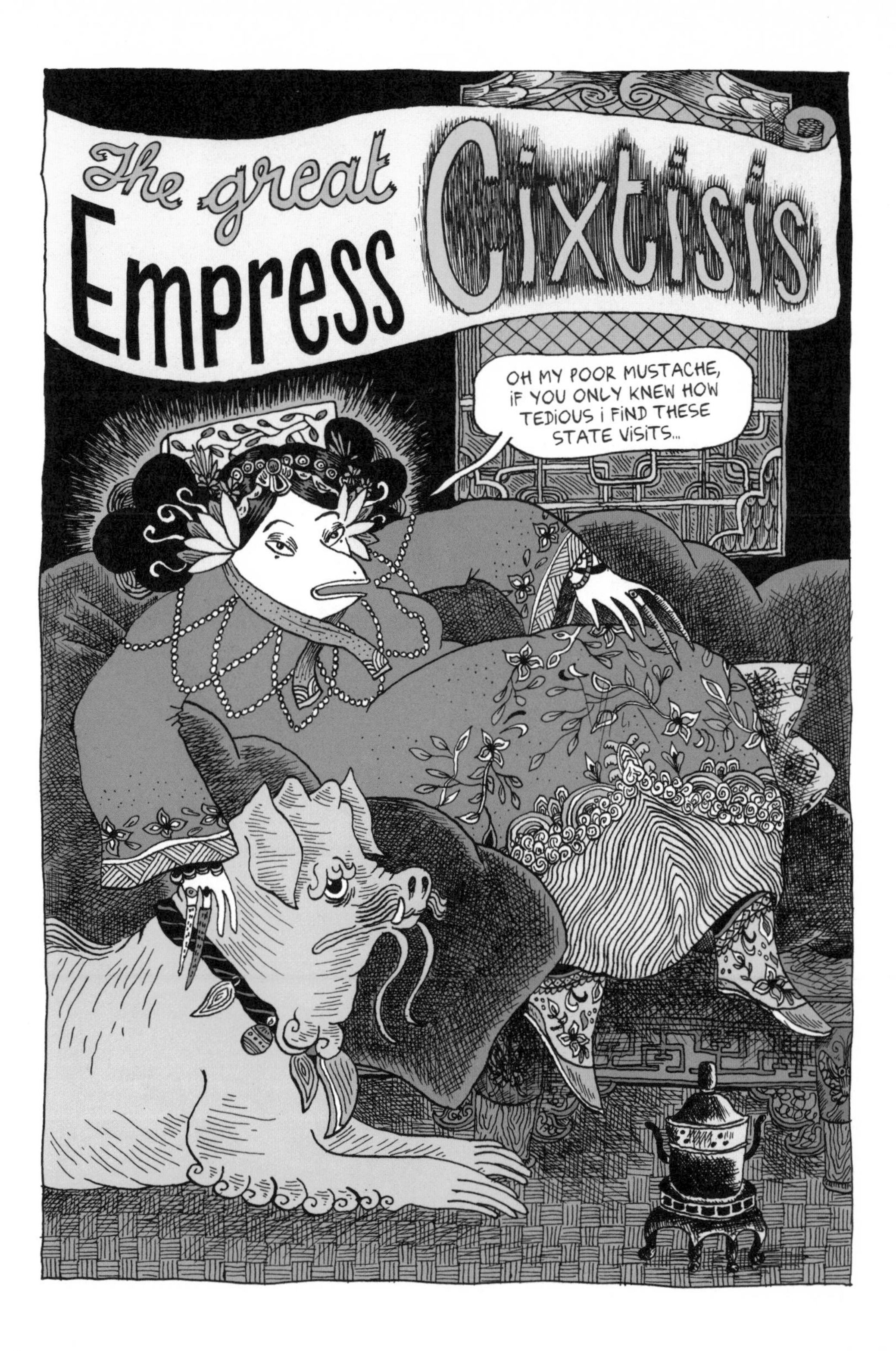
The great
Empress Cixtisis
OH MY POOR MUSTACHE, IF YOU ONLY KNEW HOW TEDIOUS I FIND THESE STATE VISITS...

THIS JOURNEY IS SUCH A BORE.
I CAN'T WAIT FOR LUNCH.

HOW LONG HAS IT BEEN SINCE WE LEFT?
FIVE, TEN... MAYBE 15 DAYS?

IT'S BEEN HORRIBLY LONG, IN ANY CASE...
YOU'LL LAUGH, MUSTACHE...

... BUT I CAN'T EVEN REMEMBER WHERE WE'RE GOING!

HALT!
HALT!
STOP!

GLORY TO OUR EMPRESS, CIXTISIS!
OH, LET'S DROP THE PROTOCOLS, LI LIAN!
DON'T BE SO FORMAL!

INSTEAD, TELL ME WHERE WE'RE GOING. YOU DON'T SEND THE GREAT CIXTISIS ON A JOURNEY LIKE THIS FOR JUST ANY OLD REASON.

WE'RE HEADING TOWARD SUFFRAGETTE CITY, IN ORDER TO MEET THE QUEEN AGLAJA.
WE STILL HAVE 100 DAYS OF MARCH-ING.

100 DAYS! INTOLERABLE! IS THIS VISIT REALLY NECESSARY?
ABSOLUTELY OBLIGATORY.

OUR COUNTRY'S FATE DEPENDS ON IT.
OH? WELL, LET'S GO ON, THEN!

YOU COME WITH ME, LI LIAN! YOUR PRESENCE WILL MAKE THIS ATROCIOUS JOURNEY MORE AGREEABLE.
... AND TIME WILL PASS MORE QUICKLY!

100 days later
SO THIS IS SUFFRAGETTE CITY? WHAT AN ABOMINABLE VIEW.

HAVE YOU SEEN THE FACES OF THE CITIZENS? GHASTLY!
THE CITIZENESSES, YOUR HIGHNESS.

THERE ARE ONLY WOMEN HERE NOW. THAT'S WHY AGLAIA WISHES TO SEE YOU...
HA HA! THEY LACK A MASCULINE PRESENCE? THAT'S NOT MY CONCERN!

AGLAIA CONSIDERS IT ALL TO BE YOUR FAULT...
PFFT HEEHEE

WELL, THEY JUST NEED A DOG OR A PIG IF THEY WANT SOME COMPANY!
I HAVE A LOT OF FUN WITH YOU LI LIAN... AND YET YOU'RE NOT REALLY A MAN.

IT'S LIKELY SHE'LL ALSO MENTION...
THE ISSUE OF REPRODUCTION...
OHHHH... YOU CAN BE QUITE UNROMANTIC.

THE GREAT CIXTISIS JUST ARRIVED IN HER PALANQUIN WITH HER ENTIRE COURT! HELLO DISCRETION!

SHE'S IN THE SITTING ROOM.
WELL... LET'S GO!

SHE DOESN'T LOOK LIKE SHE'S IN A GOOD MOOD. APPARENTLY, IT WAS A REVOLTING JOURNEY.
AND FRANKLY, WE DIDN'T PREPARE HER A GREAT WELCOME!

JUST LOOK AT THIS DREARY DÉCOR, LI LIAN! IN MY PALACE...
HELLO, CIXTISIS!

I AM AGLAIA. PLEASED TO MEET YOU.
WHAT DOES SHE WANT?
YOU MUST SHAKE HER HAND, YOUR HIGHNESS.

SHAKE HER HAND? HOW VULGAR!
DEGENERATES!

OH... WELL... UM... WHY DON'T WE SIT AT THE TABLE!

OUR COOK, DAMIEN, PREPARES THE MOST WONDERFUL RATATOUILLE!
MMM...

IN MY PALACE, I AM SERVED AT LEAST 120 DISHES EACH MEAL AND...
IN CASE YOU HAVEN'T NOTICED, THIS ISN'T YOUR PALACE, CIXTISIS.

THANKS, DAMIEN!

TELL YOUR LADIES TO HAVE A SEAT AND EAT WITH US! WE'LL BRING THEM A PLATE!
?

HAVE YOU LOST YOUR MIND?

*

OF ALL MY SERVANTS, ONLY LI LIAN IS PERMITTED TO SIT NEAR ME AT THE TABLE. FOR GOOD REASON...
HE HAS THE HONOR OF TASTING WHAT IS ON MY PLATE. IN CASE...

BUT THE THOUGHT OF POISONING ME NEVER OCCURRED TO YOU, DID IT?
N-NO! OF COURSE NOT!

TELL THE TWO YOUNG WOMEN TO GO TO THE KITCHEN WITH YOU AND LET THEM EAT.
THEY'RE NOT GOING TO HANG AROUND ALL EVENING ANYWAY.

DID YOU KNOW THAT DAMIEN IS THE ONLY MAN WE HAVE LEFT HERE?

GIVE US BACK THE MEN YOU STOLE, CIXTISIS!
IF WE CAN'T COME TO AN AGREEMENT, I AM PREPARED TO USE FORCE TO TAKE THEM BACK!

I DOUBT THEY'LL INTEREST YOU ANYMORE...
I'VE CASTRATED THEM ALL!

COME NOW, AGLAIA! DON'T FEEL SORRY FOR THEM!
I'VE BEEN WONDERING SOMETHING SINCE MY ARRIVAL.
SINCE MALES ARE SO RARE IN SUFFRAGETTE CITY...

...WHO COULD HAVE KNOCKED YOU UP?
COULD YOU FOLLOW ME PLEASE, LADIES?

COME NOW, CIXTISIS! IT'S NOT THAT DIFFICULT TO GUESS...

IT WAS DAMIEN WHO KNOCKED ME UP!

THE MOST IMPORTANT PART IS THE RAW INGREDIENTS. YOU NEED GOOD ZUCCHINIS, GOOD TOMATOES... OR ELSE IT DOESN'T TASTE GOOD, YOU UNDERSTAND?

AND NEXT, I ADD JUST A LITTLE PINCH OF SALT!
He he he
He he he

YOU WANT TO TASTE?
OH NO, NO, NO!

WE'RE NOT ALLOWED...

IT'S UM... PHYSICALLY IMPOSSIBLE!
"PHYSICALLY IMPOSSIBLE"?

YOUR EXCUSE DOESN'T SEEM VERY LEGITIMATE...
USUALLY, NO ONE CAN RESIST MY RATATOUILLE.

COME ON! JUST A LITTLE SPOONFUL...

WHY THE HECK DON'T YOU WANT TO TASTE IT?
PLEASE DON'T INSIST.
CAN WE CHAT A BIT, THEN?

YOUR EMPRESS CIXTISIS SEEMS DIFFICULT...
...BUT THEN, AGLAIA'S PUT ME THROUGH SOME STUFF, TOO!

LOOK, I'LL TELL YOU TWO A LITTLE SECRET!

I'M NOT THE FATHER OF HER BABY!
AND YET, I'M SUPPOSED TO BE THE ONLY MAN IN THIS CITY!

WE DON'T WANT TO KNOW THAT!

Kitchen
FAREWELL!
HEY!

AH! THERE YOU TWO ARE!

OFF WITH THEIR HEADS!

NO ONE WILL BE DECAPITATED HERE.
PARDON?

THESE TWO THOUGHTLESS IDIOTS LEFT TO FLIRT WITH THE FIRST MAN THEY SEE...
DO YOU FIND THAT ACCEPTABLE?

IN ANY CASE, I'LL KNOW IF YOU'VE EATEN THAT DISGUSTING RATATOUILLE!
YOU CAN'T FOOL CIXTISIS THE IMMENSE!

WELL, WELL, WELL... WHAT iF WE ALL WENT TO BED? THAT WOULD RELAX EVERYONE!
EXCELLENT iDEA, SiMONE...

DAMiEN, SHOW THE EMPRESS TO HER ROOM!

i HAVE LiTTLE TRUST iN YOUR REPTiLE!
DON'T WORRY, DAMiEN KNOWS HOW TO BEHAVE.

i'M WARNiNG YOU, YOU'D BETTER NOT TOUCH ME...

OR ELSE i'LL FEED YOU YOUR OWN EXCREMENT!

YOU SEE, SIMONE, IT'S TRUE WHAT THEY SAY!

SHE KIDNAPPED OUR MEN TO MAKE THEM HER EUNUCH SLAVES!
He he he

SHE'S STILL AWAKE...
THAT WOMAN IS NERVE-WRACKING.
I'D LIKE SOME OF THAT MILK, LI LIAN. He he he!

MILK?
WHERE DID SHE GET MILK?

GOOD MILK WILL HELP ME SLEEP WELL TONIGHT, WON'T IT?

THE MILK MUST BE PERFECTLY PURE!
YOU MAY LEAVE, DAMIEN.

OH!
Shh!

OH, GEEZ! IT WAS A CIRCUS! SHE SPENT THREE HOURS GETTING READY FOR BED AND DIDN'T STOP ASKING ME QUESTIONS ABOUT MY RATATOUILLE RECIPE...
"WHAT SPICES DO YOU USE, DAMIEN?"
THERE, THERE.
"HOW MUCH PEPPER?"
"I JUST ADD A PINCH OF SALT," I TOLD HER.

WE ARE CLEAN AND READY, O VENERABLE BUDDHA!
COME HERE, LIU...
TONIGHT, I'LL START WITH YOU.

DAMIEN, YOU HAVE TO MAKE SOME FRIES...
AGAIN?

I'M HUNGRY.

IT'S TRUE, I DID LOSE THE CROWN... I HAVE TO MAKE UP FOR IT...
POTATO

BUT SHE'S TAKING IT TOO FAR.

ASKING ME TO DO THIS EVERY NIGHT, IT'S EXHAUSTING.

"OH THAT DAMIEN! SO HELPFUL! ALWAYS THERE WHEN NEEDED!"
YOU'D THINK I WAS REALLY THE ONLY USEFUL MAN IN THE REALM!

UGH, MY SWEATER STILL REEKS OF OIL!

YOU'RE SO STYLISH, DAMIEN!
I'LL WASH YOUR SWEATER IF YOU'D LIKE!

AGLAIA! I... ER...
SO ARE THE FRIES READY?
UH... ALMOST...

HA HA! JUST A LITTLE PINCH OF SALT, RIGHT?

EVERYTHING YOU DO FOR ME ISN'T IN VAIN, DAMIEN. AND ONE DAY YOU'LL GET A PROMOTION!
I'VE GOT IT!

I'VE JUST FIGURED IT OUT... AND I'VE FOUND THE WAY TO GET RID OF CIXTISIS.

IT'S GOING TO SOUND A LITTLE HARE-BRAINED, BUT...
LATER, SIMONE!
I HAVE TO HURRY OR THEY'LL GET COLD!

ARRGGH! AS SOON AS SHE LEAVES FOR YOU-KNOW-WHERE, NOTHING ELSE MATTERS!
IT'S SO ANNOYING!

TOO BAD, WE'LL HAVE TO TAKE CARE OF IT OURSELVES!
HEY! DON'T SIT THERE. I HAVEN'T CLEANED!

DO YOU LIKE CIXTISIS'S LADIES?
HUH?
I THINK THEY REALLY LIKE YOU.

PFFF... NEITHER OF THEM WANTED TO TASTE MY RATATOUILLE...
THEY WERE INTIMIDATED!

SEDUCE THEM WITH YOUR COOKING!
OOH LA LA!

SURPRISE THEM! GIVE THEM GARLIC, FRUIT, FISH, SPICES!
I COULDN'T DO IT!
YOU CAN!

TO THE OVENS, DAMIEN! SHOW THEM WHO YOU ARE!
I'M OFF TO BED.

BISC
MÉMOIRES
D'UNE
ILLE
NGAGÉE

WELL, WELL! WHO'S THIS NOW? THE QUEEN OF FRIES!
SHUT UP, KITE! I'M NOT REALLY IN THE MOOD FOR YOUR JOKES!
CIXTISIS ARRIVED TODAY, AND NEGOTIATIONS ARE OFF TO A BAD START...

YOU'RE SURVIVORS. KEEP CALM IF YOU DON'T WANT TO SUFFER THE SAME FATE AS THE GOLD DIGGERS.
HMM... INTERESTING...

WE'RE IN TOTAL AGREEMENT, RIGHT? NO ONE LEAVES HERE FOR ANY REASON!

WHAT ABOUT OUR WIVES?
WHEN WILL WE SEE OUR WIVES AGAIN?

WOULD YOU RATHER KEEP YOUR DICK OR YOUR WIFE?
HA, HA!
IMBECILES!
HA HA HA HA!

HEE HEE! CIXTISIS WILL LOVE ME FOR THIS!

OK, I HAVE TO GO. BUT I'LL BE BACK TOMORROW... WITH FRIES.
YOU'RE TAKING TOO MANY RISKS FOR US, AGLAIA!

GRRR...
QUIET, MUSTACHE!

WAKE UP, O GRAND EMPRESS!
LI... LI LIAN?

I HAVE A SURPRISE FOR YOU.
WHAT IS IT?

TO SEE IT, YOU'LL HAVE TO BE VERY GENTLE... YOU WILL TELL AGLAIA THAT YOU ACCEPT HER PROPOSITIONS...
NON-SENSE!
YOU WON'T BE DISAPPOINTED!

I'LL DO ANYTHING YOU WANT, NAUGHTY LI LIAN!
NOK! NOK! NOK!

NOK! NOK! NOK!
DON'T ANSWER!
ENTER!

HER HIGHNESS AGLAIA WOULD BE VERY HONORED TO SHARE HER HUMBLE BREAKFAST WITH HER MAJESTY CIXTISIS.
THE MEAL WILL BE SERVED IN TOTAL PRIVACY IN THE PALACE'S SUMMER GARDEN.

THAT'S VERY GRACIOUS OF YOU AND WE ACCEPT THE INVITATION WITH GREAT PLEASURE.
PERFECT! WE'LL EXPECT YOU IN 15 MINUTES.

BUT LI LIAN! YOU KNOW PERFECTLY WELL THAT I PREFER TO EAT BREAKFAST ALONE!
NOT TODAY!
REMEMBER WHAT WE TALKED ABOUT!

AND MY MILK?!
YOU'LL HAVE IT LATER.
GET DRESSED QUICKLY — WE'RE GOING TO BE LATE!

HOW AM I SUPPOSED TO GET READY IN A QUARTER OF AN HOUR? WHERE ARE MY LADIES?
PUT ON ONLY A DRESS. I'LL TAKE CARE OF YOUR HAIR.
YOU'RE SO LOVELY AU NATUREL.

THIS IS ALL QUITE ANNOYING...
YOUR SURPRISE HAD BETTER BE WORTH THE EFFORT, OR ELSE.

SHE'S AGREED TO JOIN US! I MUST SAY I REALLY LAID IT ON THICK.
PFF... YOU KNOW I LOVE A QUIET BREAKFAST!

NEVERMIND THAT. THE SOONER YOU NEGOTIATE, THE SOONER THEY LEAVE — CIXTISIS AND HER WHOLE ENTOURAGE!

HOW DID IT GO LAST NIGHT, BY THE WAY?
YOU KNOW... THE USUAL... KITE PISSED ME OFF...
THE OTHERS WERE MISSING THEIR WIVES OR GRUMBLED THAT THE FRIES WERE COLD.

THEY'RE A PAIN... SOMETIMES I WONDER WHY WE WANT TO SAVE THEM SO MUCH.

PHILIP?
...
PHILIP IS FINE...

YOU LOOK LOVELY WITH YOUR HAIR BRAIDED LIKE THIS...
YOU THINK SO?
THE GRAND CIXTISIS WILL BE VERY IMPRESSED!

WOULD YOU CARE FOR A CROISSANT?

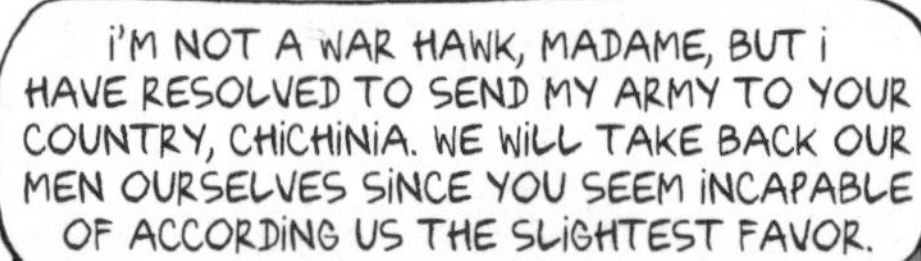
i'M NOT A WAR HAWK, MADAME, BUT i HAVE RESOLVED TO SEND MY ARMY TO YOUR COUNTRY, CHiCHiNiA. WE WiLL TAKE BACK OUR MEN OURSELVES SiNCE YOU SEEM iNCAPABLE OF ACCORDiNG US THE SLiGHTEST FAVOR.

iT iS iLLEGAL TO KiDNAP ANYONE...
AND MORESO TO DEPRiVE THEM OF THEiR... UH... SEXUAL ORGANS...

DO NOT TROUBLE YOURSELF TO SEND YOUR SOLDIERS.

IN THE NAME OF THE KINGDOM OF CHICHINIA, I FREE ALL THE MEN OF BARBARANN.

I WILL PERSONALLY TAKE CHARGE OF THEIR RETURN HOME.
WE WILL RETURN TO OUR COUNTRY THIS EVENING.

MMM...

OH, WELL, THANKS...

I WANT ANOTHER CROISSANT.

I CAN'T BELIEVE IT! IT WAS ALMOST TOO EASY!

I WAS LOUSY. I BARELY OPENED MY MOUTH!
YOU OFFERED HER A CROISSANT!
AND SHE DIDN'T SAY MUCH, EITHER...

WE CAN'T LET THEM PUSH US AROUND!
SHE CASTRA-TED A TON OF OUR MEN!

OK, I HAVE TO WRITE A SPEECH TO KEEP THE PEOPLE UP TO DATE.
I NEED TO FOCUS...

AND I'LL GO SEE HOW DAMIEN'S COMING ALONG WITH THE TWO LITTLE LADIES.
WHAT?

TRUST ME, AGLAIA!

I'VE GOT HIGH HOPES... IT WILL ALL GO THE WAY I WANT.

FAREWELL, CIXTISIS

I DON'T REALLY UNDERSTAND WHAT YOU'RE UP TO, LI LIAN!
WE HAD TO PACK OUR BAGS IN HASTE...

...YOU'RE MAKING SENSELESS DECISIONS...
AND I'M STILL MISSING MY COURT LADIES!

WE ARE HERE, YOUR MAJESTY!
WELL, WHAT HAPPENED?
YOU TWO LOOK A BIT OFF.

EXCUSE MY INTERRUPTION, YOUR HIGHNESS, BUT IT IS TIME TO DEPART...
WE WILL DISCOVER MY LITTLE SURPRISE EN ROUTE...

YOU SEE, IT WASN'T VERY FAR...
LOOK WHAT IS HIDDEN IN THIS HOLE!

TAKE CARE TO NOT FALL!
OH!
GLORY TO OUR EMPRESS, CIXTISIS!

LI LIAN, THIS IS MAGNIFICENT.

I MUST HAVE THEM.
I ABSOLUTELY MUST HAVE THEM!

LET'S TAKE THEM WITH US TO CHICHINIA!

"You love glory, Madame."

"Consider that the greatest crimes are immortalized, as are the greatest virtues...
... but what different fames they achieve in History's splendors!"*

SEE HOW I HAVE INTIMIDATED THE EMPRESS CIXTISIS!
YOUR MEN, MY FRIENDS! YOU WILL SEE THEM ONCE AGAIN!

YEAH!
LONG LIVE AGLAIA!
LONG LIVE OUR MEN!

I HOPE LI LIAN WILL KEEP HIS PROMISE.
DON'T SPOIL THE PARTY, SIMONE.

* "The Declaration of the Rights of Woman and of the Citizeness," Olympe de Gouges (1791)

SHREW!
SWINE!
YOU WON'T GET AWAY WITH THIS, YOU HEIFER!

LOUSE!
WHO IS THIS EXCITABLE MAN?
HE'S SHOUTED AND INSULTED ME FOR DAYS! I FIND HIM SO FUNNY!

THAT'S JAMES KITE.
AGLAIA'S HUSBAND.
AGLAIA'S HUSBAND?

YOU DIDN'T BELIEVE THE STORY THAT THE COOK WAS THE SIRE?
POOR KITE, HE'LL NEVER SEE HIS CHILD BORN.
Hee hee!
YOU'RE SO CRUEL, LI LIAN...

WE'LL NEVER BE YOUR SLAVES! THE BARBARANN ARMY WILL COME FREE US!
YOU WILL DIE, CIXTISIS!
I CAN'T WAIT TO GET BACK. HE'S HURTING MY EARS A BIT.

MMM, i RECOGNiZE THiS AROMA...

MY, iT iS GOOD TO BE HOME!

WE'RE NOT VERY FAR, ARE WE, Li LiAN?

AAAH, MY PALACE!
MY LOVELY PALACE.

OH!

WHAT HORROR! WE'VE FORGOTTEN MUSTACHE!

i WARNED YOU, AGLAiA. SHE REALLY SCREWED YOU OVER, THAT FAT CiXTiSiS!

COME ON, PHiLiP. THE MAiN THiNG iS THAT YOU'RE STiLL HERE...

Philip recounts the abduction

WE HEARD VOICES FAR AWAY, THEN HER HEAD POPPED THROUGH THE HOLE.
OH!
I AM THE ONLY WITNESS TO ALL THAT, AGLAIA.

I WAS CONVINCED SHE WOULDN'T FIND THIS PLACE...
WELL, YOU WERE WRONG.

I TOLD YOU THAT IT WAS TOO RISKY TO COME SEE US EVERY NIGHT. SOMEONE MUST HAVE FOLLOWED YOU.

IT'S TIME TO REJOIN YOUR COMPANIONS!
YOU WERE MISSING. THEY'RE WAITING FOR YOU QUIETLY IN MY PALACE.
SHE WANTED TO TAKE THEM INTO HER SERVICE, SO YOUR HUSBAND GOT ANGRY.
WE'LL NEVER GO WITH YOU TO CHICHINIA, YOU MADWOMAN!
NO?
DO YOU KNOW, LITTLE KITTY, WHAT CIXTISIS IS ACCUSTOMED TO DOING WITH THOSE WHO DISOBEY HER?

I GOT OUT OF IT. I HUNCHED UP LIKE THIS... SHE THOUGHT I WAS JUST PART OF THE SCENERY.

I'M JUST A ROCK NAILED TO THE GROUND. I SAW IT ALL AND I COULDN'T REACT.
NO...

EXPLAIN TO THEM, LI LIAN.
THIS ONE HERE WILL BE AN EXAMPLE. I'M SURE HE HASN'T MATURED YET!
TAKE HIM ABOVE!
DON'T MOVE OR YOU'LL SHARE HIS FATE!
AAAAH!
THAT CRY OF PAIN, WE ALL KNEW WHAT IT MEANT.

I TOLD CIXTISIS THAT IT WAS DAMIEN WHO GOT ME PREGNANT...
...

WELL... I'LL GO EXPLAIN TO THE OTHERS THAT...
...THAT YOU LIED TO THEM AGAIN AND NOW THEY'LL NEVER SEE THEIR HUSBANDS AGAIN.
DON'T FEEL OBLIGATED TO TELL THEM ALL THE DETAILS.

GLORY TO OUR EMPRESS!
THANKS.
HE CAN HAVE THEM BACK WHEN HE DIES, SO HE CAN BE BURIED "WHOLE."
NOW, BE GOOD AND FOLLOW ME, ALRIGHT?
YOU'RE A SWINE, CIXTISIS!
THE WOUND WILL TAKE MORE THAN 100 DAYS TO SCAR OVER.

SEE YOU LATER, PHILIP.
GOODBYE, AGLAIA.

OH!

COME HERE, DOGGY...
COME
HERE!

WELL THEN! YOU'RE LESS
CALLOUS THAN YOUR MISTRESS.

SIMONE!

WE HAVE A
HOSTAGE!
CIXTISIS CARES
ABOUT HER DOG,
RIGHT?

A FAX FROM AGLAIA? SAY THAT AGAIN, LI LIAN?

IN BRIEF, SHE WILL RETURN MUSTACHE TO YOU IF YOU RETURN HER MEN TO HER.
OH!

A DOG FOR HUNDREDS OF MEN!
WHAT A SIMPLETON!

MUSTACHE IS A CHARMING LITTLE BEAST, BUT I WAS STARTING TO TIRE OF HIM...

THESE HERE ARE MUCH MORE AMUSING. I'M COUNTING ON KEEPING THEM FOR A WHILE YET.
CRETIN! FLOOZY!

BE NICE, KITE, OR I'LL PUT YOU AT THE TOP OF THE LIST.
YOU'RE A NUTCASE!

CIXTISIS REFUSES TO TRADE!
ZZZZZ

GOOD GOD! SHE WROTE A NOVEL!
IT'S ALL GOING WRONG...

I HAD A PLAN, BUT IT'S TAKING A WHILE TO IMPLEMENT.
DINNER IS READY.

WE HAVE TO DECLARE WAR ON CHICHINIA.
BUT HOW? WE DON'T HAVE AN ARMY!
IT'S GETTING COLD.

YOU LIED TO CIXTISIS WHEN YOU SAID BARBARANN HAS AN ARMY.
BUT THERE REALLY WAS A BARBARANN ARMY BEFORE!

I SEEM TO REMEMBER THEIR CORPORAL WAS NAMED SABINE...

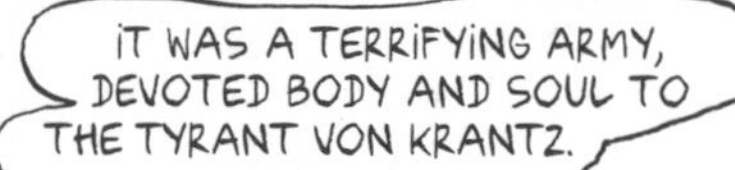
IT WAS A TERRIFYING ARMY, DEVOTED BODY AND SOUL TO THE TYRANT VON KRANTZ.

THEY LOST THEIR MASTER WHEN YOU ROSE TO POWER.

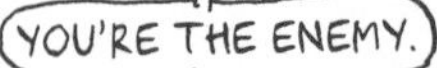
YOU'RE THE ENEMY.

CIXTISIS WRITES THAT IN 100 DAYS, OUR MEN WILL HAVE ALL LOST THEIR... VIRILITY.

...AND THAT KITE WILL BE THE FIRST IF HE DOESN'T WATCH HIS STEP!

WE HAVE TO FIND SABINE AND HER ARMY... AND CONVINCE THEM TO FOLLOW US.
SABINE...

YOU KNOW SABINE?

IT'S A LONG STORY... IT... IT DOESN'T MATTER WHAT OUR CONNECTION WAS...
DURING MY EXILE, I LIVED IN A LITTLE HOUSE.
AND?
AND ONE DAY I SAW HER! SHE PASSED BY MY WINDOW!
BUT SHE RAN AWAY... I DON'T KNOW WHERE SHE'S HIDING.
SHE WAS WEARING THE CROWN ON HER HEAD.
MY CROWN? ON THE HEAD OF A STRANGER? ALSO, I WAS THINKING THAT...
YES... IT SMELLS LIKE FRIES!
SNIFF SNIFF
OH! FIND HER, MUSTACHE! FIND HER!
FOLLOW HIM!
I'LL WAIT HERE... GIVEN MY STATE...
Much later...
HE FOUND SOMETHING!

What do you want with us? Are you the police?
WE DON'T WANT TO HURT YOU. WE CAME TO SEE SABINE.
She's inside.
I'LL LET YOU GO IN ALONE. YOU SEEM TO KNOW HER BETTER THAN I DO.
PUT YOUR SWEATER BACK ON.
SO ANYWAY... HAVE YOU LIVED HERE LONG?
DAMIEN!
We have nothing to do with each other anymore, you know that!
SABINE...
OUR COUNTRY NEEDS YOU!

* See "The Song of Aglaia"

Sabine goes to war...
Damien was quite proud of his persuasive power.
The Valkyrie fries were hidden across the country.
At Sabine's call, they finally emerged from their hideaways.
They lived by plundering for years, at the fringes of society.
Their rage over being conquered was unleashed.
They once again became the fearsome Barbarann army.

They arrived in Chichinia in less than 100 days. Soon,
they will begin the assault on Cixtisis' palace. Sabine
tells herself she is ready to fight. She is jubilant.

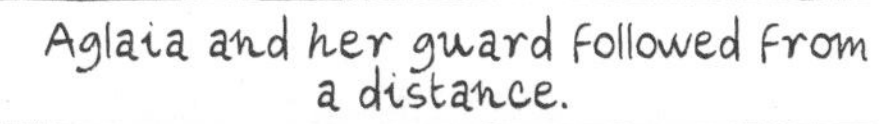
Aglaia and her guard followed from a distance.

SABINE LOVES A GOOD FIGHT. SHE MUST BE HAPPY SHE'S NOT STILL HOLED UP IN HER CAVE.

HMM... I DON'T LIKE THIS.
MY PLAN WAS MUCH MORE... PACIFIST.

DID YOU REALLY GIVE THEM THE JARS?
YES. I DID JUST WHAT YOU SAID.

THEN AGLAIA WANTED TO FIND SABINE. COME ON... MAKE UP YOUR MIND...

For Feng Liu
For Mi Zhen

WELL?

THIS IS DELICIOUS... IT... HAS FLAVOR.

WE SHOULDN'T. SHE'LL KNOW.
DAMIEN SAID IT WAS INOFFENSIVE.

Meanwhile...
GIANT FRIES AT THE PALACE DOORS? HOW AMUSING!

WE MUST DEPLOY OUR ARMY AS WELL, O VENERABLE BUDDHA!

DO IT, LI LIAN. DO WHATEVER YOU BELIEVE IS RIGHT. IF AGLAIA WANTS A WAR, SHE'LL GET IT!
AND THEN I'LL TAKE HER OUT!

WAR BREAKS OUT

The enemies are resilient...

The losses countless...

it's chaos.

STOP! STOP THIS MASSACRE!
TOO LATE.

THEY'RE ALL DEAD.
HOW HORRIBLE.

BUT CIXTISIS IS STILL ALIVE.

I SAW THEM AT THAT WIN-DOW, HER AND HER EUNUCH. THEY WERE WATCHING THE BATTLE WITHOUT EVER INTERVENING.
GOD! IT'S A SLAUGHTER.

AND NOW, IT'S THEIR TURN.
SABINE! NO!

IT'S YOUR FAULT MY ARMY WAS DESTROYED. LET ME FINISH THE JOB!

YOU WANTED TO GET YOUR MEN BACK, BUT i'VE LOST ALL MY FRIENDS.

i WILL KILL THE GREAT CiXTiSiS. THAT WAS MY MiSSiON, WASN'T iT?

DO NOT TROUBLE YOURSELF.
AGLAiA, YOU HAVE WON.

CiXTiSiS iS DEAD.

POiSONED... ALONG WiTH HER TWO LADiES...
HOW DiD YOU GUESS?

SHE COULDN'T HAVE DiED FROM POiSON. i TASTED ALL HER DiSHES...
...EXCEPT FOR THE MiLK, OBViOUSLY.

I OWE YOU AN EXPLANATION.
I'M RESPONSIBLE FOR EVERYTHING.
CIXTISIS LIKED DRINKING FENG LIU AND MI ZHEN'S MILK.
OH, YES! SHE LOVED IT.
BUT THE MILK HAD TO BE PERFECTLY PURE!
OF COURSE!
CIXTISIS'S FAVORITES FOLLOWED A STRICT DIET, FOR FEAR OF SPOILING THEIR NECTAR.
THEY ATE ONLY BLAND FOODS.
BUT THEY DREAMED OF SALT, PEPPER, SUGAR!
WHEN YOU FORBID SOMETHING, IT BECOMES MORE ATTRACTIVE.
MAYBE.
I ASKED DAMIEN TO PREPARE A CONCOCTION... WITH STRONG FLAVORS...
IT'S TRUE. I COOKED THEM FISH SOUP WITH ONIONS, GARLIC, AND SPICES. I IMPROVISED. IT WAS A CHANGE FROM RATATOUILLE.
I ADDED BLUEBERRIES AT THE LAST MINUTE.

THOSE WEREN'T BLUEBERRIES...
?
I REPLACED THEM WITH BELLADONNA BERRIES.
WHAT?
IT WAS LATE... YOU WERE DRUNK...
YOU DIDN'T NOTICE THE DIFFERENCE.
BELLADONNA IS A FATAL POISON.
THE POISON PASSED INTO THE MILK, AND CIXTISIS DRANK IT.
THE PROCESS WAS RATHER SIMPLE.
THE COURT LADIES COULDN'T SURVIVE EITHER.
YOU'RE DIABOLICAL!
CIXTISIS WAS A BITCH, BUT I KILLED TWO INNOCENT PEOPLE BECAUSE OF YOU!
MY PLAN MEANT THAT THERE WOULD HAVE BEEN ONLY THREE DEATHS!
I DID IT TO AVOID THIS CARNAGE!
WHY DID THEY WAIT SO LONG TO OPEN THE JARS?
IT DIDN'T WORK.
WAR WAS DECLARED BEFORE MY PLAN SUCCEEDED.

YOUR SIMONE IS VERY STRONG.
WHAT AM I GOING TO DO NOW, WITHOUT MY EMPRESS?
LI LIAN...

BUT YOU'RE FREE NOW.
I CAN'T EVEN PLEASE A WOMAN!

I DEFEND THE RIGHTS OF WOMEN BUT I CAN ALSO UNDERSTAND THE SUFFERING OF MEN.
WHAT CIXTISIS DEMANDED FROM HER SLAVES IS INTOLERABLE.

REBUILD YOUR COUNTRY. ENSURE THAT NO ONE IS CASTRATED IN THIS COUNTRY EVER AGAIN.

YOU'RE LUCKY. A LARGE PORTION OF YOUR FLOCK IS STILL "INTACT."

I RETURN THEM TO YOU.
THANKS.
AGLAIA!

You can win the war and not cry victory.
They returned to Suffragette City in silence.
Some men were dressed in the traditional robes of Chichinia slaves.
Those men were recognized as the ones Cixtisis didn't spare.

And life returned to normal...

SIMONE & AGLAIA

AGLAIA & PHILIP

KITE & HENRY

AAAH! IT'S GOOD TO BE BACK HOME!
HEY, POUR ME ANOTHER LITTLE DRINK, HENRY.
THAT REALLY WAS A CLOSE ONE, OLD FRIEND!
YEP!
AND THAT GREAT CIXTISIS DIDN'T STOP PISSING ME OFF, REPEATING THAT I WOULD NEVER SEE MY CHILD. PFFF
WHAT THE HELL DO I CARE?
IT'S NOT MINE.
SHE'S HAVING IT WITH THAT BIG ROCK OVER THERE!
AGLAIA CAME TO SAVE US, DESPITE EVERYTHING.
YEAH... AGLAIA THE SAVIOR. THE PEOPLE ARE CRAZY ABOUT HER. SHE'S MORE POPULAR THAN EVER.
SHE'S OUR QUEEN...
WIF!
WHAT ARE WE GOING TO DO WITH THIS MUTT?
HE'S SO UGLY...
HE LOOKS LIKE A PIG.
WUF?

SABINE

COME ON NOW, SABINE, GIVE IT BACK TO ME!
NO!
I ONLY LOANED IT TO YOU. I'M STILL THE QUEEN.
LET'S PLAY POKER FOR IT.
BUT... I DON'T KNOW HOW TO PLAY POKER.
TOO BAD FOR YOU!
SABINE!
HHH...
YOU SHOULDN'T RUN WHEN YOU'RE PREGNANT.
THE IDEA OF IT! IT'S YOU WHO PUT IDEAS INTO HER HEAD!
I PROMISE TO BRING BACK YOUR CROWN, AGLAIA.

DAMIEN & PERSEPHONE

The Chichinia Empire, dead asleep...

FANTAGRAPHICS BOOKS INC.
7563 Lake City Way NE
Seattle, Washington, 98115
www.fantagraphics.com

Translated from French by Jenna Allen

Editor, Spot Letterer, and Associate Publisher: Eric Reynolds

Book Design: Anne Simon and Keeli McCarthy

Production: Paul Baresh

Publisher: Gary Groth

Thanks to Delphine, Perrine, Guillaume, Damien, and Renaud.

www.instagram.com/anne0simon/

ISBN 978-1-68396-221-2
Library of Congress Control Number 2018967041

First printing: July 2019
Printed in China

BIBLIOGRAPHY

"Mémoires d'un eunuque dans la Cité interdite" by Dan Shi, Piquier, 1998. (French Translation)

"Mémoires d'une dame de cour dans la Cité interdite" by Jin Yi, Piquier, 1998. (French Translation)

ALSO AVAILABLE BY ANNE SIMON:

The Song of Aglaia (Fantagraphics Books, 2018)

The saga of Queen Aglaia and the citizens of Barbarann will continue in *Boris the Potato Child*.

THE MEN OF SUFFRAGETTE CITY

☒ *Checked box indicates castration.*